The Days

Also by M.A.C. Farrant

Short Fiction

Novels

Non-Fiction

Plays

* Available from Talonbooks

The Days

Forecasts, Warnings, Advice

M.A.C. Farrant

Talonbooks

Talonbooks
278 East First Avenue, Vancouver, British Columbia, Canada V5T 1A6
www.talonbooks.com

First printing: 2016

Typeset in Scala
Printed and bound in Canada on 100% post-consumer recycled paper

Cover illustration by Catrin Welz-Stein, catrinwelzstein.blogspot.com
Cover design by Chloë Filson
Interior design by Typesmith and Chloë Filson

Talonbooks acknowledges the financial support of the Canada Council for the Arts, the Government of Canada through the Canada Book Fund, and the Province of British Columbia through the British Columbia Arts Council and the Book Publishing Tax Credit.

LIBRARY AND ARCHIVES CANADA CATALOGUING IN PUBLICATION

Farrant, M. A. C. (Marion Alice Coburn), author
     The days : forecasts, warnings, advice / M.A.C. Farrant.

Short stories.
Issued in print and electronic formats.
ISBN 978-1-77201-007-7 (paperback).
     – ISBN 978-1-77201-008-4 (epub).
     – ISBN 978-1-77201-009-1 (kindle).
     – ISBN 978-1-77201-010-7 (pdf)

     I. Title.

PS8561.A76D39 2016   C813'.54   C2016-902340-0
                                               C2016-902341-9

For Terry

... the days were very long
while the years were very short.

—Louise Glück

Contents

2

3

I

Four-Day Forecast for Wendy

I

You have a keenness to never let your running mind rest.
A keenness to be emotionally important.

You love dancing while wearing a bowtie and are
not allergic to glee.

But you will never applaud a legend in the
unmaking. Your dad, the retired banker, for one.
His aging narrative has grown side effects.

Yesterday he was spotted exposing himself at a busy
intersection while wearing see-through pantyhose
beneath your mother's curry-coloured coat. This caused
mild excitement among passing motorists. The police
were called. A witness described your dad as "not
having much to show for himself." He was quietly
delivered home.

In light of all this, your becoming an astrophysicist
doesn't seem like such a big deal today.

2

Today you are in the Original Mystery business, a former
bride hoping to penetrate the story, deliver the goods.
Elements of a leaping terrier appear, and devoted goats,
elephants, as well as flat, floating fish. A festival of
washing dishes, cooking, hauling garbage, weeping, and
laughing appear.

Mostly you are rushing from one beginning to
another declaring, "Doesn't the world look stunning?
It almost feels natural!"

It's hard to describe the look in your shiny
chocolate eyes.

3

On this day you will mention to Gary, your husband of twenty-nine years, that you wouldn't mind being your family's head of state. You come from a long line of matriarchs, you'll explain, and so your request is not an unreasonable one. Furthermore, you will say, "The men in your family do not become heads of state, ever. They tend to drop back to their own devices and drink Scotch in the corner of the living room with the cat on their lap."

It will be late afternoon when you broach the subject with Gary. He will receive this as Good News! He'll be in the garden shed smoking his daily joint. He'll be sitting on the old white leather chair he dragged out there and he'll be looking at you pleasantly. You, on the other hand, will be breathless. Nevertheless, you will tell him what's on your mind.

Gary will be quiet for a long while after you speak. He'll be staring at the dust on the shovel. Finally, he will say, "If that's what you want, Wendy ..." And grin.

4

Today your dog, which is wearing a red vinyl jacket and is tied to the boulevard tree outside the thrift store, will decide to end things. His name is Rusty, and suddenly, he feels like he's dragging a rusty anchor.

This is because he now understands the truth of his situation: you don't really love him. It's what he's suspected for some time – that, for you, being with him is like being in a prison. Because he, Rusty, is never going to grow up and go to school and get a job and support you later. That very quickly he's going to become an old dog and possibly an expensive and cranky one.

When you come out of the thrift store he can read the truth in your eyes. Even though you say, "Thank you so much for waiting for me," he knows it's a lie. Your mind is elsewhere. You'd sooner walk by him and visit the cat in the pet shop down the street.

Every dog should have a boy instead of a fifty-six-year-old woman, he thinks.

This Year

- the dog will have six hundred friends

- almost everyone will lead a charmed life and spend it singing

- no one you love will get hurt, though some of us worn-old will disagree with this

- many will wear so much gold for good luck that no one will offer them guidance

- hair will be mostly styled for its hypnotic value

- everyone will follow forecasts, warnings, advice

- everyone will be part of the chorus, the ubiquitous hum

- everyone will plan to enjoy the next twenty-seven years

- everyone will get their picture taken with the President

Backup Chorus

- We are three nameless women harmonizing behind the male lead.

- Three TV goofs walking into walls with ladders.

- A quartet of optometrists singing "Wait till the Sun Shines, Nellie" on board the doomed flight in Kurt Vonnegut's *Slaughterhouse-Five*.

- A string trio covering Green Day over there by the subway exit.

- Five old women knitting together in a storefront to attract business.

- We are Janet saying to Elaine, "I was beautiful once and everybody loved me."

The Cinderella Problem

You have a fondness for sweeping floors and raking leaves. You are happiest alone or when getting your hands dirty. You've often thought you'd make a good Cinderella. You like shoes and would consider a prince with a foot fetish as not a bad catch. You like a fancy-dress ball as well as the next person.

Many of these attributes have been put forward over the years but you have never been chosen. It's beginning to look like you will never star in a fairy tale.

Your ugly stepsisters were actually good looking.

Your stepmother did the best she could.

The Chicken Remedy

If you need to peck ceaselessly at worrisome things,
and it's becoming a problem because you are pecking
so much that it's causing turmoil in the lives of others,
wear red contact lenses.

This remedy has been inspired by chicken farmers.
Red lights in the henhouse will decrease a chicken's
high, the one they get from pecking each other to death.
Red contacts will do the same for you.

I am a chicken that knows this.

National Craft Day

I've sculpted this clay figure. It's tiny, four inches high, but only has three legs because I ran out of clay. It can't stand on its own. It could be mistaken for a frog because I painted it green. But I like it. And I want other people to like it too.

How many people do I want to like my sculpture? How many people do I want liking it before I am satisfied that it is really liked? Can I put a number on that? I wouldn't say no to a thousand people. A thousand people liking my sculpture would be pretty good, though more would be better. And Facebook "likes" don't count because I want my sculpture to be liked for longer than a few seconds.

Another thing – do I have to be alive while people are liking my sculpture? I ask this because "decades" are no longer an option for me. Do I want people liking my sculpture, then, when I am just-about dead? After I am dead? When I am long-dead?

Oh my God! How dead is long-dead these days?

Hands on the Wheel

There is no law forbidding your dad from taking his
electric train set with him when he's buried. Many people
have taken things with them after they die, the idea being
that they've still got their hands on the wheel, so to speak.

Bob Marley took a Les Paul guitar and some weed.

Miles Davis took his trumpet.

Tiny Tim took his ukulele and some red tulips.

Harry Houdini took a packet of letters from his
mother. (There was no escaping his mother.)

Roy Rogers took his cowboy hat, his dog's ashes,
and a pair of riding gloves.

Frank Sinatra took a bottle of bourbon and
a pack of Camels.

My mother-in-law took her full-length mink coat.
She wore it.

My grandmother took a deck of cards so she could
continue playing solitaire.

My uncle took his dog Buddy, who'd died a week
before. Buddy had to be dug up and reburied.

Then there was my father. He was a quiet man, but
also a man of action. He wanted a roll of quarters with
him in case he found a pay phone. To call home, he said.

Dream Come True

I remember my dad telling me about growing up in Winnipeg, Manitoba, when he was a kid, and how his grandpa retired off the farm and moved in with my dad's family. And his grandpa lived out his days with them. That's what happened to my dad's parents and blah, blah, blah. That's what you did back then, you looked after old people, blah, blah, blah.

My dad's grandpa died on the couch, with two loaves of bread and some peanut butter on the coffee table and a bag of apples beside him. He had twenty-eight dollars in his pant's pocket. The family had left him for a few days to go to a hockey tournament in Brandon.

Fortunately, things are different now. It's become vogue to put your parents in a nursing home or whatever, or find them a place in a retirement community. Now you can get on sooner with your post-parent life.

Summing Up

I'm an optimist by nature so still have many friends.
And I've stayed true to the end. I've been coming back
like an affectionate robot for decades. I haven't lost it
yet – water-skied fully clothed or worn a clown costume
to town on a Tuesday afternoon.

I'm a sweet guy.

I've loved the handsome heads and hefty vaginas
of many. I've loved drinking Scotch against existence
rushing by, and attending undertaker conventions
because it wasn't me yet.

But you don't want people to know how long you've
been around. If they do, they will think, "Well, that's
long enough. Pull the plug on him. He's had his chance."

I hope my end is sudden. I want people to say,
"Who said he could leave the party?"

Vibe

Oh there you are, dear. I thought you were dead.

The Hearse Driver Speaks

Once a gentler, more respectful public was the norm. A funeral procession was escorted by police on motorcycles. People stopped and took off their hats, put their hands over their hearts. Cars pulled over. For a few moments onlookers paused in reflection. It was like a Norman Rockwell painting – among them a shopkeeper in a brown apron, an old woman in a blue coat, a freckle-faced boy with his mouth hanging open.

Not so today.

Today a funeral procession with a police escort will not be seen unless you are a hero or a major politician. Today the driver of a hearse manoeuvres in traffic like everyone else. We get no special treatment. In fact, it is not unusual to have someone in a car cut me off and then give me the finger as I watch them drive by. Several times I've driven a hearse that's been pelted with pop cans. I've had people yelling obscenities at me, making rude gestures from the side of the road.

What do they think is going on? Do they think it's a scene in a movie?

They need to understand that death is driving by. That when the inevitable happens to someone they love, it will bring with it a degree of sadness. They need to understand that, for example, of course they will miss Shannon, but that life's a bitch, and then you move on. That Shannon is dead.

Vibe

Don't be too moody in school these days
or they'll put you on pills.

Keep Calm

Even while the woman in your dream lingers in your bedroom doorway smoking a cigarette.

And the man holding a clipboard and who looks like William S. Burroughs announces that the reality genre is cooling.

And original poems, stories, phrases are written, read, and forgotten, meaning that your masterpiece has eluded your grasp again.

And the rumpled bed covers in the half-light look like a woman curled and weeping.

It isn't you. It's your imagination.

Couch Lock

Every time I see superweirdos on the bus I embrace them. This is because I've come to realize that, like me, superweirdos naturally want to overthink things and analyze, like, the meaning of life, and that the only way to do this is to disengage from those around them and let the messages come through. I figured this out one time I was high on the narcotic analgesic drugs I was taking for my broken foot.

So I started getting into this state of couch lock, which is doing absolutely nothing while sitting on the couch. Like, nothing, nothing, like, less than nothing. Doing nothing feels like riding a wave, and then you feel another wave coming, and you paddle hard and you hit it. You spend the day doing this, and the next day it's the same.

Doing nothing, I've had moments when I am, like, Whoa! And moments when I'm a little dazed and can't believe this is real life.

Yesterday the message was that I am getting better at singing. Today the message came in the form of a memory, the one where I got heckled at my own wedding reception. Ashleigh, my ex, was off dancing when a drunk jumped on the table and yelled, "You're nothing but a joke, Brandon, a character in a Woody Allen movie!" I must have looked like such a loser.

Old Days

When I was seventeen I heard a noise coming from the backyard and went to investigate. That's where I found Peter, the boyfriend of the woman who owned the house. He was lying in the driveway in his boxer shorts with a knife sticking out of his chest. It was that kind of a neighbourhood.

We lived in the basement suite. My dad was always yelling at us to close the door. "The door's not an asshole. It doesn't shut by itself!"

You want the obvious truth? Death was a bit overwhelming, and talk about decay made me sick. So I thought, well, everything. It was, like, maybe Peter died for love, maybe not. But hopefully his girlfriend would get a stack of money to help her with the change, going forward.

The yard next door was where I went on a daily basis. I was constantly there with Lisa. I'd sit on her back steps and sing "Sherry, Sherry baby." She had a passion for vegetable soup, but I always knew eventually she'd come out.

Calendar

Now and then you will find yourself thinking of time as a calendar in a late-night, black-and-white movie you saw when you were ten years old. You and your father on the Colonial-style couch in the den.

Near the end of the movie the screen cleared and a calendar tacked to a wall appeared. Each page on the calendar contained a single number representing a single year. One by one the pages came loose and fluttered to the ground. A pair of birds flew in to take the pages away. Cartoon birds like in Disneyland.

You felt unease at the speed with which the years disappeared, and how easily. Your father must have sensed your mood because he said, "It's showing the passage of time. Loretta Young was twenty when the movie started, and now she is fifty. You see that, don't you?"

You take a deep breath of terror and say yes.

Doris Grant Day

Doris Grant was a home economist who invented
a brown bread that didn't need yeast or time to make
it rise. As a result, the people of England didn't go
hungry during the Second World War. They could make
the bread between air raids.

Where brown bread was concerned, Doris Grant
said, "If you love your husbands, keep them away from
white bread. If you don't love them, cyanide is quicker
but bleached bread is just as certain, and no questions
asked." She said loaves of white bread should be
dropped over Germany.

Think of Doris Grant while the bombs of bad news
continue to fall on our heads.

Secretary Day

Pushing upwards means wanting to dance where you're
not supposed to.

Perseverance means wearing your secretary suit like
a legend in your own time.

You're kidding? means there is seldom joy in filing.

Top means work is cry-worthy but extraordinary.

Bottom means departure towards small things as
a keeper of secrets.

Sixth place means it feels like God rather than you who is
making a fortune being successful.

Fifth place means a banana suit for the off-hours.

Fourth place means a hallowed task and a singing mouth.

Third place means your body is like a devoted goat.

Second place means it feels like a journey of
bodily insides.

First place means it furthers one to wear the gorilla mask.

No blame means everyone is written into your story for
a reason but you will never know how the story ends.

Gordon Lightfoot Day

Oh, this day is tough. It finds me in my older years
sitting at my desk. As usual, I've been clawing at ways to
keep the universe exciting. One way I've found is to heed
the words of Clint Eastwood: "Never let the old man in."
Or in my case, the old woman. Another is to listen to
Gordon Lightfoot's songs again, the ones about moving
on. Altering their meaning a little. I hope he doesn't
mind. So that moving on can also mean not getting stale.
Not letting the dust settle.

It's Supposed to Be a Fun Deal

Everyone's so nervous these days. Not me. I've been wearing my party clothes all week. On Thursday evening I'm hosting a tap-water gala!

Though Hillary says hosting a gala during a time of austerity and normalized decline is a weird thing to do. And Mother says one should be careful of tap water. And David says I look like the Second Coming in my long white apron.

But I wonder. Are we not about to have a keen new perspective on things? For example, the fifth of May has been declared National Prayer Day across the United States of America.

When I saw the *Mona Lisa* at the Louvre, I was, like,
meh? Because I'd seen the picture a million times.
On jigsaw puzzles, posters. So it was, like, I waited in
line for this?

In every picture she's wearing the same dress.
She has no eyebrows or eyelashes. Her hair lies flat on
her head. She's sat on the same chair for five hundred
years and still doesn't know when her husband, the
silk merchant, will return from China. Off-picture,
her mother-in-law's bleating about the lack of beer in
the larder. The roof's sprung a leak. The servant girl
is pregnant again. The second plague pandemic is
happening. Millions are infected or dead. A lucky few
struggle to find a last safe corner for humanity.

There are so many things like that you've seen so
many times before.

Ritardando

When you wake up on the morning of July 2 you will be looking, as usual, for that deep, great, plus-size model of life. You won't find it. Instead, you will find a day that is situated at the exact midpoint of the year.

This balancing of the year always occurs at noon. If you want the second half of the year to carry on in much the same way as the first half did, that is, with you alive and kicking, then you will need to do some balancing of your own. The easiest way is to straddle a teeter-totter for a few minutes, one in a park, or one of your own making.

This balancing is called a ritardando, a sacred pause in the flow of things. Failure to pause and balance could result in your feeling like you don't even belong here.

Interestingly, even though the second half of the year doesn't yet exist, it still weighs as much as the first half. Mixing existence and non-existence together like that is a feature of the arcane law called Cheat and Transformation, by the way.

Also of note: July 2 is World UFO Day. Expect to watch the skies this night. There are bad things out there, and they are close.

Annual Day

Annual Day happens once a year and it is never good.
This year the date is March 2.

As usual, you will attempt to ease its passing
but this will be futile. Nothing will help. Not playing
Madama Butterfly in the morning with the windows
open. Not making yourself feel glad about the clouds.

By afternoon you will be sitting over tea like
a chalk statue with blank eyes, thinking: Today
existence is something to subsist in, breathe, vegetate,
and be converted to.

Then you will lie down and face the wall.

Later, even the stars will look dull.

How We Live

At any moment a fog bank of evil intentions can appear.
Knowing this, we traffic in distractions.

I wear a candelabra on my head, or drink wine
holding the glass with my toes, or do a thing with my
grandmother's flapper beads. This seems to help.

You go around wearing a false head, one of a giant
seagull. Just because we live near the beach.

And we attend many festivals to keep ourselves
buoyed, the latest one being in celebration of large
numbers: Sixty thousand real estate agents in the
City of Toronto!

But mostly we get pissed, start a fight, and get
bounced from the tea shop.

Today's Letter

It's a beautiful life we have, but sometimes not so much.

There's Aiden. We had to accept his building cars. He's says he's an artist now who only cares about what he's creating. He'll cut up your car without asking.

And Anthony. We had to understand and respect his choice. If he wants to go to Tibet or Nepal on some kind of spiritual journey that's his business, even if he is an atheist.

And Ben. He was on TV overcoming his demons, and reaching out and seeing the supreme love over the whole world. All Praise to the Lord for that.

Otherwise, it's the same old same old.

Ed made twenty-four in cribbage.

We put the cat down.

Darla says her baby's a real private person.

Mother's Advice

Never listen to anyone who says that clowns are stupid and you should become a venture capitalist.

Never look for deep structure in a bowl of oatmeal.

Avoid chomping on gum. If you substituted mashed potatoes, would you find chomping acceptable?

Search out people to laugh with when things become unhinged.

Stay alert. The road is in a hurry.

And remember, if you are not in the red playroom of pleasure with some naked flesh in your face, the experience of an afternoon is much like that of any other afternoon.

It is always fun until someone pokes an eye out.

Father's Advice

If you're looking for a phrase guaranteed to ruin a first date, say, "I know this sounds crazy, but I think I'm falling in love with you." Likewise, never take a date to couple's therapy. And when your special day rolls around, never say, "It's my birthday, I can kill a kid!"

It is better to ignore the bass beats in life and dance instead to fragments of rhythms. It will make you look like you're having an epileptic seizure, but so what? Like Frank Zappa, you will be saying, "Oh, this is the great new way!"

And each day you should ask yourself: Have I checked for infectious diseases? Played the banjo? Breathed mindfully. Known which mouthwash causes cancer?

Because this is it, the community of fleeting moments. And it's true, the real story is even more incredulous than the one you tell yourself.

The Sailor's Advice

Learn to navigate your days. Never set your course by the moon. Pay attention to the stars. Lean into the wind.

Remember, there is always the swift pace of passing years. You will feel this acutely while trying to grab the day by its throat.

Grit your jaw.

Steady as she goes.

Grandma's Prophesy

There will be violence, there will be sex, there will be brothels in every town.

Waves of tears will continue to flow; death will remain a timeless character. For the vast majority of people this controversy will never go away.

The generational differences between the young and the old, however, will remain a source of amusement.

Brad and Angie will call it quits. They love each other intensely but want other things out of life.

You, on the other hand, will never get everything you want. Your father will continue to take his helping of wives. Pay attention! Your mother will continue to shovel snow.

Advice Ancient and Modern

To ensure that a change in life or in love will be good, the ancient advice is to throw hot stones against the door where you are living. Besides providing you with temporary good luck, this action will also cause all liquids in the vicinity to flow more freely. Rivers will become fast flowing; heavy rain will be unleashed from suddenly ashen skies; your blood will quicken its course through your body, causing your face to flush, your muscles to strengthen, and your energy level to soar.

You will need this energy. Because along with good luck comes bad luck, often in the form of malevolent spirits that will tamper with your liquid moments, causing your thoughts to become like rooms filled with landmines, causing gleefulness to vanish, dread to be restored.

The modern advice says there are several strenuous things you must do to ensure that bad luck doesn't gain the upper hand, but so far we don't quite know what these strenuous things might be.

Perhaps there's a list somewhere.

Maybe you can find it.

Or figure one out.

The only advice I know is to wear yellow and hold your breath.

Vibe

You're only as good as
your last YouTube video.

2

How Nice Was My Reply?*

Did it make you feel singular, weird,
beautiful, and primal?

Did it make you believe you were going down
the right road?

Did it make you forget the eternal questions:
Who am I? Where am I? What am I doing here?

Was it as nice as a mother confessing to a radio
psychiatrist that her teenage son has an obsession with
cat characters?

Did it make you feel, Oh my God, I am amazing?

Was it like, Oh man, do I admit this? I have always
wanted to wear an Elvis jumpsuit?

Did it make it easy for you to integrate back
into reality?

Was it like a pie-eating contest? The first mouthfuls
are tasty but now you're sick of it?

Was it army-booted, shave-headed, and pierced in
places people are talking about?

Did it make you wonder if you are not
just a collection of microbes, or a fat-chance
physiological system?

Was it more like, I wish your stupid morning had
drowned in a puddle?

Was it more like, the edible garbage is out back
in the alley?

Automated reply from online retail store after complaint was answered.

Deep End

You've been on a Jack Kerouac fantasy trip for years, looking to become the next keeper of imagination's flame.

First stop – the abandoned Zen motel in Mesa, Arizona, where you filmed yourself reading by the light of your emptied mind. After that it was any small town with an audience. You had a collection of one thousand haiku-like novels to hustle, each one not more than twenty-five words long. You couldn't help asking anyone who came by, "Don't you just love the cover?"

Those lines you drew in the sand and thought would remain forever? Well, the tide just came in and washed everything away.

Frog Chorus

- Oliver declared his love for me while gazing at the stars, and this got me thinking: Who is Oliver, and how did he get into this story?

- As ever, nature did not have command of the words needed to answer. There was just the cool moon and me with the heart of an oak and nothing to say.

- I find consolation in the fact that tomorrow some of us will know where our next meal is coming from. And most of us will get caught up in that story, the one about suspense and survival.

- All of this is foretold in the calendar of spectacular dreams, that tells us each day begins with, "Holy, there's something going on here!" and ends with a goosebump factor.

Not Every Day Will Be the Best Day of Your Life

This is my story, yes. But I would also say, okay, I enjoy
my food and life in general. And I always bounce back.
I'm like a punching bag that gets pushed to the ground
and pops up again. And all my power comes from my
reasonable brain, something Manny Moss appreciates.
There's no lack of appreciation when it comes
to Manny Moss.

There's a plot, right?

Well, there's a heady combination of bawdiness and
some really good existential jokes.

*Nowadays the audience is very plot-literate so it's hard
to have unexplained events.*

Does it count that Manny Moss and I are flawlessly
flawed but in a not-too-obvious way? That for years
people thought we were having perfect moments when,
in fact, many of those moments were sour?

You decide.

Well, we did our fair share of moping ...

*Ah, another Woody Allen movie. Lots of critics.
No audience.*

We indulged in hysterics at the back of a movie
house. Does that count? And one time Manny Moss
pulled down his brother's sweat pants at breakfast
because his brother was over-staying his welcome.
What about that?

*Never underestimate the public's appetite for
devilish plots.*

I think mine is more of a love story. It's, like, if you
can't be together you'd rather call it a day. But then, other
times, at night, I sing Nat King Cole songs in the alley, to
no one, really ...

Yes, well. Thank you. What's your name?

Marion.

Thank you, Marion.

It's Like There's a Wormhole in the Universe

We have these things in common. Once we were young.
Once the ordinary universe felt exciting and bittersweet.
We were teen heroes battling teen villains. And every
summer going to Midway Park beyond the highway.
Remember the rides and stomping on mustard packets?
I accidentally sprayed a girl's white jeans with the
yellow stuff.

Back then it was a crazy stamina experience.
We were like an early draft of a person, where they
sketch out a skeleton and only later add on the details,
like pigment, crow's feet, worry lines.

Like understanding the score.

Now we weep easily. We're troubled sometimes.
We make mistakes. Now it's "Do not ramble, eat
your oatmeal."

What's the difference between being seventy and
eighty years old?

Ten minutes, we say.

Deaf Day

I heard a deep high, I mean sigh.
    I had a mixed message instead of washed lettuce.

History of the Kitchen Sink

You call out the kitchen window, "Gerald, are you there?"
     When he doesn't answer you return to the sink, the
suds, and the stew pot. Your husband is missing again.
Sitting in the fifth wheel with his sex books probably.

Story

Mimi, meanwhile, jumped into her white Miata and revved the engine. She was about to leave, I knew, for that place where superheroes communicate with each other in an abstract and poetic way.

Punk Kitchen

For some time now you've been wanting a Punk Kitchen.
No one else has a Punk Kitchen and owning one, you
believe, will raise your esteem in the eyes of your friends.

To make this happen, to turn your kitchen into
something anarchic, you've hired legendary punk
artists Matthew Hollow and Hammer Lee. They've been
working all morning on an installation but have taken a
break to confer. They can't figure out how to transplant
the bindweed they've been growing on your bedroom
carpet. The bindweed's destined to cover the kitchen walls.
They are absolutely twisted in knots over this problem.

You've been looking up the regulations in the
Punk Handbook, hoping to help. Surprisingly, you're
finding the regulations exciting. They're like a poem and
a dream. There are so many points of entry. So many
ways to dissemble meaning. You're enchanted, which is
something – as the owner of a Punk Kitchen – you know
you should not be.

The regulations say nothing about bindweed
on kitchen walls, however. When you tell Matthew
Hollow and Hammer Lee this, they both say, "The fuck."
And then Matthew Hollow takes a baseball bat to the
fridge and Hammer Lee tears the cupboard doors off
their hinges.

You remain absorbed in the Punk Handbook.
It contains many quotes to fall in love with. *I have fond
memories of floating down the Ganges on chunks of flesh*, by
Jello Biafra. *It's pretty hard to be artistic when you're middle
class*, by Lisa "Suckdog" Carver.

Day with Clouds

A cloud shaped like a blind terrier with its mouth open
floats across the sky towards a stick on the far side
of an adjacent cloud. It's a slow process taking ten
minutes. By the time the terrier reaches the stick, the
cloud has transformed into a breast and the dog is now
biting the nipple.

Nearby, eighty elephants stand inside a large
cumulous cloud, holding it up. Eighty elephants is how
much a large cumulous cloud weighs. The elephants
are made of condensed water vapour. They are not
lighter than air but they stay afloat because of convection
currents from the sun-warmed ground.

Soon enough the elephants will change into
something else, a flying saucer, a slew of running nuns.

I am on the ground thinking how clouds are like
people locked in a time machine, bluffing their way from
one adventure to the next, something I do about every
ten minutes.

Day When Thoughts Became Audible

It was caused by something David Suzuki said in
a lecture: "I am in the death zone now."

Some of us were waiting in cars at traffic lights
or in lineups at grocery stores when we read his words
on our phones. Some were at ball games or outdoor
festivals. Many of us were at home with a glass of wine,
but all of us were reeling.

Like a bad new virus, David Suzuki's remark
caused panic.

Even though he later apologized and said it was
taken out of context, that he was speaking solely about
himself and not the planet, no one believed him.

As an antidote to the panic some of us tried
speaking words of bland observation like: *An old man
with a gnarled right hand crossing the street. A large woman
in a car fixing her hair in the rear-view mirror.* But it was
useless. The quiet and ordinary world had disappeared.
As a result, some of us got drunk and drove our
minivans into concrete walls.

Vibe

It was so special to see the endangered and beautiful coral in their aquariums.

Viewing them helped us disentangle our minds from ruminative thoughts, destructive emotions, and impulsive and addictive behaviours. It also made us want to own a hat decorated with coral. And a coral-coloured scarf, a coral shade of lipstick, a pair of coral-coloured pyjamas.

We hadn't realized the degree of fandom there would be for endangered coral. Honestly, we don't think we have ever been so excited!

The Chorus at 3:00 A.M.

—   I'd be curious to see who's still around in 2034.

—   You're going to see all the beloved characters.
    There's going to be Vera and Gladys and Kate and
    Betty and, of course, Brenda.

—   I like the new gal. She's smart, funny, surfs, sings.

—   Beloved characters are not magical, you know. They
    take a lot of work. Hearts are broken along the way.

—   It's today and tomorrow, and don't get cranky.

—   And then you try to do better and you never do better.

—   Well, you can't pawn a tattoo.

—   I once pawned my wedding ring.

—   I once tried to honour soldiers by placing a flag on
    every grave, but I ran out of flags.

—   You might actually do what you think is the best thing
    in your life and nobody notices.

—   It's not all naked women and pastries, you know.

—   All I care about is playing the trombone.

—   I thought I was going to be Mr. Universe and start my
    own vitamin line.

—   If Shakespeare walked in here right now, would he
    feel at home?

—   What is one sausage's quest to discover the truth
    about his own existence?

- My favourite part of the whole thing is the little groupies standing out there.

- Personally, I like to sit back, smoke a cigarette, and laugh for six minutes.

- Well, it's certain we'll be thanked forever with regards to inventing the igloo.

Vibe

I decided it was too expensive for me to go to the grocery store – a luxury. I was focused on surviving so I ate stuff from the Dollar Store – mayonnaise, soup base, vegetable oil, chick peas, cinnamon hearts.

I was never sick. I never felt bad. I never went to the hospital.

That's not what I expected.

Today's Mystery

I said to Banksy, "Let us pause for a moment to consider the deeper meaning of your work."

We paused.

"Okay," he said. "That's long enough."

The Marilyn Statue

"I feel stretched and pulled and chewed and spat and trodden on," she says.

We can barely hear her because her mouth is twenty-six feet above our heads. She's wearing her flying-up dress from the movie *The Seven Year Itch*, and everyone's taking pictures of her underpants, which are white with lace trim. A person stands between her legs and points the camera upward. The question still being asked is, Will we catch a glimpse of her giant vulva, or will we not?

Manny Moss takes a shot of her underpants and the answer remains no. Then he climbs onto her high-heeled foot, the left one, and hugs her leg. I snap and snap. The red paint on her big toe is chipped.

All day tour buses filled with bejewelled seniors from Los Angeles come to gaze at her concrete immensity. At night she's lit with red floodlights. She's a big girl, weighing thirty thousand pounds. From close-up, she appears to tower above the surrounding mountains.

"I'm this town's strip mall," she says, but no one is listening.

In the afternoons, the Palm Springs high school choir sings the national anthem on the lawn where she stands. Then Pastor Fred in a black track suit climbs onto a picnic table and blesses the shutter-clicking crowd.

The Finish Line

Just moments away from becoming an eighty-five-year-
old former superhero resting in peace, the Lone Ranger
gallops towards the finish line, an arc of red, yellow, blue,
and green balloons strung across Palm Canyon Drive in
Palm Springs, California.

The waiting crowd wants one last encounter
with the Lone Ranger's textured and sensational and
fantastic world.

What a day! It's unbelievable to see all these
celebrities arriving in helicopters.

The high school band is playing the *William
Tell Overture*, the Lone Ranger's personal theme, and
cheerleaders are standing on each other's shoulders
chanting his name. And there's Tonto looking adorable
with the couple's twin poodles, Brad and Bianca.
And there's the animal rescue people with the crane.
If Trigger survives the ride it'll be a miracle, they say.

The day's a hot one, thirty-two degrees Celsius.
Volunteers are handing out free Gatorade.

We're on the sidewalk watching the scene from
webbed lawn chairs, flags and drinks in hand.

We couldn't love the Lone Ranger more.

When you cross the finish line you drop dead.

The Space Station Astronaut Speaks

It gets pretty insane up here talking about our T-Zones.
T for taste, that is. "Am I eating a melon or a lamb chop?
Oatmeal or gravy?" The humour is definitely not the
multi-cam sit-com variety. More of a one-two punch.

Mostly, we just fumble around. We don't do anything
spectacular, which is kind of funny, considering. At one
point someone punches Robin, which is not an easy thing
to do when you're floating, and his head hits the control
panel. Randy says, "What's the sound of one head hitting
a control panel?" and this cracks us up because it's kind of
an accidental-Buddhist thing to say.

Our favourite game is called "Trap the other guy
with a crazy old gal who never stops talking." Obviously,
crazy old gals are in short supply up here so we take
turns dressing up like one and hanging, literally, in the
shower stall, the idea being, who can entertain the other
person for the longest period of time?

Come evening, we broadcast the day's events back
home. Everyone there thinks we're pretty cool because
we genuinely like each other, love each other, and I think
that translates.

Then just before bed Randy pulls out his guitar and
sings something spiritual about the big emptiness we're
rolling through. It gets cozy, then, like the last two days of
camp when you haven't done the water skiing yet, or the
archery, and you don't want to leave.

We've Been in This Position for Decades

"Did you see what the dog threw up this morning? A bit of bone she got out of the garbage."

"I'm leaving in five minutes. For my credit-counselling appointment."

"What did you do with the broom? I want to get at those cobwebs."

"I am leaving."

"You know, I'm getting sick of the colour red."

"I could have told you that."

"Is Boyd going to trim the tops of the cedars or just the sides?"

"I don't know. Look! There's a hummingbird at the feeder."

"There's a mouse on the living-room rug. The cat must have brought it in last night. I thought I heard something."

"I am leaving now. I am going into the closet. Maybe this time I'll find the exit."

"Watch out for Jay in there. He'll pop out even though he's supposed to be dead. He'll be standing beside you and he'll have the axe."

"I know. I have the gun."

Vibe

Bucket list? The only thing left is to see
how long we can run the string.

Today's Letter

Life is pleasant here in Oz, apart from people stabbing
and shooting each other, as they are in other countries.

Lots of people are on welfare. But restaurants,
coffee shops, and clothing stores are doing well. Wages
are high. Bethany made eight hundred dollars one
weekend while on hols from uni.

And Steve made some money in the stock market
so everyone's treating him like surfing royalty.

Patricia's in a shut-down phase. Bob is dead.

There's always something. ˙

It's usually the weather for us. We seem to
attract torrential downpours, wildfires, or flash floods.
This time one of our trailer's wheels is wobbling in
a really abnormal way.

There Are Times When You Are Forced to Respond to Things

You've invested your family's savings in cocoa-bark mulch, a garden mulch that's been described as "mouth watering" because of its chocolate smell. You believe you can make good money importing and selling this product locally. But your ultimate plan is to funnel whatever money you make into the non-profit organization you have just created and which you are calling *Arrows for Loving Kindness*.

While waiting for your first shipment of cocoa-bark mulch from Central America, you've launched a crowdfunding appeal for start-up donations in support of the *Arrows for Loving Kindness* campaign. You've included a proviso that whatever money you collect must come from a place that connects with your spiritual aim.

You are not exactly sure what *Arrows for Loving Kindness* is meant to do, but you have faith that the universe will soon tell you.

Little Person

Don't make eye contact with a baby. They're like cats.
They know who doesn't like them. I made that mistake
at Emily's tea and soon enough her baby was hanging
onto my leg. So I had to pick it up and hold it while
it squirmed and drooled and everyone made cooing
sounds. It was awful.

"There you go," I said, after exactly one minute,
and handed it back to its mother. But it returned for
another assault, dragging itself across the carpet like
a demented seal.

"Nope," I told it this time. "I am off-off-off."

I'd made a point not to sit anywhere Kyle and Emily
might have had sex, choosing a rickety three-legged stool,
reasoning, probably not here.

Mainly, I wanted to shout at Emily, "You had sex
with Kyle, like, fifty times before he left me?"

But instead, I said, "Pass the cookies," and
hated their baby.

The Uncomfortable Zone

I was driving fast around a hairpin mountain turn and naturally a wheel hit the shoulder and the car plunged over the cliff and landed upside down in a ravine. When I crawled out I didn't recognize a thing. There was mist that could have been drifty people, and there was jungle music going thump thump thump. I thought these things made sense because my middle name is Alice and I had just gone down a hole of sorts.

I was unhurt but the music was getting on my nerves. I now had a mission. Find the volume control and turn it off. It was when I was thinking this that help arrived in the form of the writer, J.G. Ballard. April 19 is the anniversary of his death and since this was April 19, his appearance was another thing that made sense.

J.G. Ballard told me to breathe deeply. He said the thumping sound was my beating heart and that I should think very carefully about wanting to turn it off.

Adrift

"The moon and the sun are travellers of a hundred generations," wrote Haiku master Matuso Basho in his seventeenth-century travelogue *Narrow Road to the Deep North*.

"The years, coming and going, are wanderers too. Spending a lifetime adrift on boat decks, greeting old age while holding a horse by the mouth – for such a person, each day is a journey, and the journey itself becomes home."

Memo to self: Find a horse's mouth.

Green Water

I was searching for a day that would feel like, Welcome
to the party! For years I'd heard I'd find one if I crossed
the Great Water. All I had to do was close my eyes
and click my heels together three times. So I did that.
My shoes were rubber boots, but suddenly they had
wings. When I opened my eyes I was standing on a
beach before a large tropical fish tank. Several fish
cruised in the green-coloured water.

Then I noticed an old man lying curled up and
sleeping at the bottom of the tank. I could tell he was
sleeping and not drowned because air bubbles rose from
his mouth and broke the water's surface.

I knocked on the glass and the old man woke up,
looked at me, and climbed out of the tank. A small, wet
Oriental man. He squeezed water from his jacket and
said, "Well?"

"Not very," I said.

He squeezed more water into a cup and gave it
to me to drink. Soon after I saw pink birds perched in
a blossoming cherry tree. The old man grinned and
climbed back into the tank.

And here I am, gawking at the pink birds, still not
knowing what it all means.

Day Off

The external world is offering much today, including
a day off from your self and its necessities.

So step outside with the dog. You're going for an
afternoon walk, one where you will soon become aware
of the March sun. It's weak this time of the year but not
so weak that it won't light up the daffodils from within.
You'll notice this, and also that the air smells like wet dirt.

Outside, you'll soon discover, is where all kinds of
things are happening.

In your neighbour's yard, for example, there's a
display of bronze statues that he made himself. Wolf,
bear, eagle, fish, and a four-foot pelican about to
take flight.

Along a side road you'll see leaf buds, hear
birdsong, watch as sparrows chase one another through
tree-top branches.

You'll look down and notice the many pink-
grey worms on the road's surface. The worms are
there because of the heavy rain last night, which has
caused the dirt where they live to become flooded.
You'll understand this. The worms are flood victims
searching for drier ground.

Immediately, you will know what to do. Finding a
strong twig, you'll carefully transport the worms, one by
one, to the side of the road.

Save as many worms as you can before a car comes.

The Complicated Solo

Last Saturday you left Pam, your wife of forty-two years, for Donna, the woman you met at the bowling alley last winter. Donna is nineteen years younger than you. You've been seeing her at the Emerald Isle Motel on the highway for some time now.

It's Pam's fault that you're leaving, you think. Pam had said, "For God's sake, Richard, find something to do!" So you joined the bowling league.

Now you're telling Pam, "You don't have to be young and handsome and thin to have good things happen to you."

It's like you are speaking to her from behind a podium. You're feeling spirited and wise.

"Every person, man and woman, has to be prepared to dance a long and complicated solo at the end of their lives," you say.

Within weeks your house will be sold and the assets divided. Pam will buy a condo, new furniture, up her bridge games, get the kids and grandkids onside, and register for ballet and flamenco lessons in the fall.

Then time will pass.

You and Donna will take many trips together, including ones to Mexico, California, and Hawaii. There'll be an Alaskan cruise and a train trip across Canada. One summer you will drive to Halifax to see Donna's mother. All the while you will be happy. The sex will stay good.

When, a few years later, you are put in a home, try not to worry. A certain Margaret there will like the look in your eye – the way you smile at her when she passes your private room.

Vibe

I can tell you without a shadow of a doubt that everything
is normal. This is because spring this year is phenomenal
and breathtaking, much better than we'd expected.
There's the sense that we're masters, we're special, we're
in growth-mode. Hopefully, we will share feelings about
this with our loved ones, and also the joy of eating.

Other than the fact that people don't stay here
forever, and even with sickness and murder and
getting old and strange weather, there really is no
downside to life.

The champagne is in the fridge, you say?

Here's me in my tuxedo, jumping up and down.

French Connection

When you reach the two-hundred-and-eighth day of the year it will be July 27. On this day, in 1890, painter Vincent Van Gogh shot himself in the chest. He did this in one of the French wheat fields he frequently painted. He was thirty-seven years old and died two days later. His last words were, "The sadness will last forever."

Also on this day, in 1946, writer Gertrude Stein died in France while being operated on for stomach cancer. She was seventy-two. A year later, the American novelist Katherine Anne Porter writing in *Harper's* magazine will call Stein's work the "long drone and mutter and stammer of her lifetime monologue," and refer to her "tepid, sluggish nature, really sluggish like something eating its way through a leaf."

For the rest of us still living, even the sluggish ones, July 27 will be like all the other days, which is to say, a combination of breath and panic and glory. There is not much we can do about any of this.

Dylan Thomas Day

How many hens go through life looking for their fathers
in the faces of strangers?

    Wondering, "Is that him? Could he be my rooster?"

3

Dream Lover

He's a flower, a rolling lawn, a philosopher, and, finally, a poem. Anything else is second rate. He can jump, kick, flip, and stunt, and this has an effect on me. So I am positive, living the show. You totally get this point?

Well, he chases me. He's a six-foot-tall good time. There are forms of free-floating sex and sounds loud enough to excite. It means being carried around. It's all about the smiles.

Who doesn't think they deserve humanity?

I love how much he loves the universe. He isn't just blowing on embers. He's a raging bonfire himself.

"Marion," he says, "you are such a pleasant form of exercise."

"Don't pinch me," I tell him. "I don't want to wake up."

Festival in the Kitchen

The kitchen is a place of ambition and fear and
desperation and a whole bunch of other things.

The kitchen is where you make friends with strange
and unusual vegetables.

And every day you prowl it with your insect zapper
looking for pantry moths.

Dream about turning garbage bags into confetti.

Never forgetting the egg's integral role in all of this.

The kitchen is where you perfect your kitchen language.

Making a fist signals your teenage son to close the
fridge door.

Holding your hand horizontally after mashing
pinto beans means you've had bare-bones times before
and survived.

Fluttering your fingers signals the last pot has been
scrubbed and you can now go to bed.

Placing one hand on the collar of your shirt
and leaning against the stove means you need help.
Oh, with everything.

The kitchen is where your formative years were spent.
You were like some strange kitchen nerd because you
loved washing dishes and nobody quite got you.

Your mom would make little fritters out of cardoons,
a type of thistle, so yes, you ate thistles.

Your dad was trying your whole life to impress
you by making Sunday pancakes, even when he
was hungover.

A recipe: You take chicken soup and shove it
up your soul.

The kitchen is where you display the prize you received in Grade 12 for Home Economics.

It's a bronze coin encased in a glass cube, small enough to hold in the palm of your hand. In the middle of the coin a pair of woman's hands hold up a modest house.

Rays are engraved around the house to indicate splendour. On the back of the coin the inscription reads, *Future Homemakers – Towards New Horizons.*

You won this prize for not losing your apron six years running.

The kitchen is where you now occasionally give demonstrations on how to wash dishes the old way. Strangers gather to receive your instructions on water temperature, quality and quantity of dish soap, the correct order of washing (glasses to pots). There are discussions concerning the controversy around rinsing, yes or no, hot or cold, and, finally, an in-depth presentation on types of tea towels, linen being the best.

You are an acknowledged expert in the field.

You neither strip completely nude nor wear an apron when you give these demonstrations.

You have bottoms on and wear pasties.

The kitchen is where friends often gather to drink wine and taste your cheese melts, your crusty crostini. This happens towards the end of the party, when it's midnight and the music's still loud.

You realize that this might be as good as life gets. You may cry your eyes out over this revelation, but you will still be happy, weird as that sounds.

That's what a festival in the kitchen does. It's about discovery and understanding.

Like a theory of the universe.

The kitchen is the place for cute tricks. On command, Bryce will roll over and play dead. Then it will be your turn. You will beg for your supper. One pork chop, a hill of peas, a glass of soda water, rice.

Doing these things will prove that you're a good girl and he's a good boy.

Later in your kitchen, you will play with a pair of hot chestnuts. Bryce, the owner of the chestnuts, will say, "Whoa, Christine, I get where you're coming from!"

Treats all round.

The kitchen is where you are often funnier than usual.

Bryce knew he was in the presence of someone a little crazy – and incredibly talented – when he married you. But today you are off the dial. It's pretty magic.

You've stuck a lit Roman candle between your teeth so you won't cry while peeling the onions.

You're going to see if it works.

Old Wives' Day

This is the day you realize you've become an old wife.
It's because your husband, Owen, has given you an
electric can opener as a thirty-second anniversary gift.
And because the celebration dinner is the two of you at
the Dairy Queen – Flamethrowers, Diet Cokes, a shared
Oreo Blizzard – after which you ride home in silence
sucking an orange Life Saver. Okay. So be it.

But consider this. Being an old wife can be a cause
for joy because you can now put your stamp on each day.
From here on you'll be able to add to the world's store of
tales, sayings, and remedies. And there's a good chance
you'll become valued, even prized, because of this. You
will soon learn that being an old wife changes all the
pieces on the table.

The only problem is that being valued can mean
you're in danger. This is because old wives are becoming
a scarce item. Maybe divorce or disinclination are the
reasons, but there are fewer of you participating in the
long-haul marriage. As a result, old wives have become
a rarity. People have taken to running off with them.
They've become a cultural product, valued like argon
crystal, or a horse coloured amber champagne. There
is now this amazing phenomenon of old wives just
quietly disappearing.

If Owen is worried about theft, tell him it's unlikely
you will be taken. As an old wife you're a pretty standard
model, small and blonde, and you're not shy and have
a big mouth. You also wiggle your finger a lot, like an
old cat woman, and you know what that means. Cats can
suck the breath from a baby.

Dorothy Parker Day

On August 22 we honour Dorothy Parker for her corrosive wit. Born in Long Beach, New Jersey, on this day in 1893, she came to prominence as a writer, reviewer, and satirist while working for the *New Yorker* magazine during the twenties and thirties of the last century. "Those were the terrible days of the wisecrack," she wrote. "There didn't have to be any truth."

There still doesn't have to be any truth, which is why August 22 has been designated as the one day of the year we can say corrosive things and be free from public censure. Dorothy Parker was reputed to have said corrosive things every day of her life, including the fact that she loved dachshunds better than men.

> "The first thing I do in the morning is brush my teeth and sharpen my tongue."

> "I require three things in a man: he must be handsome, ruthless, and stupid."

> "Beauty is only skin deep, but ugly goes clean to the bone."

> "Tell him I was too fucking busy – or vice versa."

On Dorothy Parker Day we wear wool suits and little hats, smoke with cigarette holders, and have a liver-coloured dachshund on a lead. We wander about being bored and sullen and sad and nasty.

"If you can get through the twilight you can live through the night," she said.

Come evening we toast her with whiskey sours, her favourite drink – bourbon, lemon juice, and sugar over ice. She was drunk most nights. When a reporter asked her if she was going to join Alcoholics Anonymous, she said, "Certainly not. They want me to stop *now*."

She died of a heart attack on June 4, 1967, her preferred words for an epitaph being, *Excuse My Dust*. Her ashes remained unclaimed in a lawyer's office for seventeen years.

Roddy Doyle Day

– The Queen of England's brought out this exclusive line of clothing.

– What?

– She's calling it *Reign Wear*. There's a whole campaign going on. On account of her being the longest reigning queen ever.

– No way.

– Haven't you seen the ads? It's coats and hats and gloves and shoes. All matchy-matchy pastels and kind of, you know, dumpy-looking.

– Jesus.

– My mom's a big fan. She got the works in Celeste Green. Don't you love that name? She got the matching hanky too. Likes waving it around.

– Like royalty in a car? Like standing on a balcony?

– Like standing on the bow of a submarine.

– Before it goes under.

– Ha. Yeah. My mom says the hanky's symbolic and waving it and wearing the Queen's clothes fills her with pride.

– I guess, at her age.

– There's these white curly wigs you can get too.

– I've seen them. Cotton tops.

– Looking like the Queen of England's starting to be a big deal.

– Is there a website?

- Of course there's a website. I'm thinking of an outfit in Bare-Bones Yellow. It'd totally go with my rubber boots. I'd look like the Queen in her Wellies.

- Are you being weird? What would you do in it? Visit a hospital? Tour Australia?

- I don't know. Maybe I could wear the outfit when I'm having tea at home with friends. That's what my mom does. All of them sitting around in their Queen clothes getting wasted on tea with gin. My mom even wore the clothes when she took Chalky to the vet. People there were super nice, she said, on account of what she had on. You know, respectful.

- I'm not dressing up like the Queen of England to get respect.

- Why not? My mom says the outfit makes her feel regal, makes her feel she could last another sixty-two years. She says wearing the Queen's clothes calms the central nervous system, like yoga. Lets her laser-focus when needed, like when she's walking around nodding at strangers.

- Carrying her little matchy purse over her arm.

- Yeah. It's a cutting-edge look.

- We're living in a time when this is happening?

- We are. But the clothes, wearing them we get to share in the Queen's *savoir faire*. They're supposed to make everyone dream.

- Sounds like a feel-good type of deal to me.

- Well, who doesn't want that?

Guys in the Chorus

– For the most part being in the chorus is interesting
   and provocative work. It's stimulating. It makes me
   think. It's fun too. And I've got a good day job, play
   golf, barbeque.

– The female chorus is quite raunchy.

– I realized early on that things in that department
   could change at the drop of a hat. So I make an effort
   to have my life filled with things I love to do. I've
   stayed true to that approach.

– A lot of nights I feel like the mayor of Venice!

– The female chorus is still a mystery to me. It's like
   you have to be two halves of a single person.

– I got to do a little dancing with Amy, which was pretty
   amazing. This was before I became used to being
   someone's husband.

– They go in for sexy costumes, the female chorus.
   That's something.

– While we go in for banana suits and gorilla masks.

– At least I'm not your typical bad guy running around
   yelling at people, "Get in the car trunk, now!"

– Me neither. I not a thrill-seeker. I'm more of
   a snack-seeker.

– Actually, a lot of fascinating stuff still happens on
   my back porch.

– Ah yes.

The Cashier Speaks

"Don't take too long to evaluate your existence," the
cashier at Super Foods told me. She was older, had silver
rings on every finger and on both thumbs. I was buying
frozen peas, a tub of ice cream, dish soap.

"The universe is big and you are small," she said.
"You are not as big as the moon or the planets."

"Yes," I said. "I've heard that."

She scanned the peas.

"There are a hundred billion galaxies out there
bigger than you."

"Yes." I looked around. The old guy in line behind
me was holding a boxed apple pie.

The cashier said, "Those galaxies have nothing to
do with time, you know. We're the only ones who have
time. That'll be twelve twenty-eight."

I gave her my card.

She said, "Some of us were very surprised when
we heard all this. Some of us started getting really sick
and had to be evacuated by helicopter." She handed me
the groceries. "I wish things had worked out but it looks
like nature's changing the script. We're a controlled-risk
species. We're just blowing raspberries at this point."

She turned to the old guy. "Isn't that right,
my handsome?"

He grinned.

Outside, a helicopter was about to land. Another
one of us had fallen, this time in front of Maxine's
Shoe Emporium.

Vibe

I want Dad's final resting place to be a piece of art and not an urn. A ceramic jar or a porcelain egg, on par with someone who gets a really nice casket. Only you get to see it all the time. It's not rotting away underground somewhere.

If you're going to put someone on your mantel, you want them to look nice. You want people to say, "That's beautiful!" not "Oh, that's Ken's ashes."

Seeing His Ex at the Wedding

"Dredging up the past is like brushing your teeth with a steak knife," he said.

"Now I'm going to get wasted and head back to the motel alone."

Some Days You Just Can't Talk ...

Because your tooth is hurting. It's not attached to
a smile, and, what is more, you are without a dentist to
call your own. The only help is the dental clinic where
others like you groan with abscessed teeth and show the
whites of their eyes and clutch take-your-turn numbers
like lucky charms.

Where occasionally there's a slight turmoil when
the receptionist acts like a bartender and says, "What'll it
be?" And people cry out, "Gingivitis! Aphthous ulcers!"

Where after something like a year goes by she
hollers "Four hundred and thirty-two," which causes
some poor fuck to shuffle through the door marked
This Way Please never to be seen again.

You decide to wait outside on a bench and try to
forget your inability to chew or speak.

Your sister-in-law, Karen, has tried to help.
She found some forty-year-old tabs of acid sewn into an
heirloom poncho and you've taken two but they're not
working the way you had hoped. For example, there are
all these flattened bodies of women in blue housecoats
lying on the sidewalk like paving stones, some of them
still clutching their jaws.

You'd hoped to turn into a monarch butterfly.

Dog Days

What are you saying, Bonnie? I am saying:

- That Uncle and Aunt's dogs came to their ends
  sooner rather than later.

- That Sandy, the bald one, who could dance on
  his hind legs, was deaf and wandered.

- That he choked on a snake.

- That a drunken spaniel named Bubba came next.
  That Uncle fed him beer instead of water and that
  Bubba was one of those mean drunks, grrr this,
  grrr that. He died of a fatty liver.

- That a retriever cross named Sylvia, who was all
  tidy between the lips and had long-haired legs was
  next and that Aunt was sold on her for a while. "You
  get love where it lands," she told Uncle. "Look! The
  d-d-d-d-dog kisses!" Then Sylvia chased a woman on
  a bike and had to be put down.

- That once, when I was nine years old and they didn't
  have a dog, Uncle squatted on the kitchen floor
  with Aunt beside him on her hands and knees and
  said, "Sit up and beg, Bonnie. There's a good girl."
  I climbed onto the counter for laughs but instead
  I got my nose smacked and was put outside to think
  things over. And I am still thinking things over.

- That meanwhile Grandma moved in and started
  calling out to anyone who would listen. "All the way
  to the end of the damned universe," said Uncle.

- That a stray German shepherd came by and
  this was the dog Aunt really fell for. They called
  him Harry. He could pee on command, and play
  Behave Yourself with Aunt.

- That not long after Harry's arrival, Grandma curled
  up by the stove like a shivery chihuahua and died.

The Importance of Discovery

Now that I've turned nineteen, my parents have decided that this friend of theirs would be fun for me to meet.

"I'm an advocate of this man," Dad says. "He may be somewhat smarmy and the means he uses may be a little gross, but I think in some ways his ends are decent."

"Does he work at the sex shop?" I ask.

"Well, honey, he does," Mom says. "He owns it. But don't let that stop you. Getting to know Bruce will be a very interactive, very fresh experience for you. Plus, he's always working on new and better ways for people to enjoy themselves."

The sex shop means a lot to my parents. Something magical happens there between persons who are truly amazing, they say.

Mom is anorexic and Dad is 322 pounds. I find that kind of juxtaposition pretty amazing too.

"We want our lives to be real. Not, 'Oh look, the puppets are having sex!' We want it to have a happy ending. We want to feel like we're in a good place.

"Furthermore, we are struggling with real issues and we don't know the answers to them. We feel the world has cast us off and we're in this weird, confessional bubble. We want to plant an explanation but we don't know what's going on.

"It can be a very difficult and hard and cold journey.

"Your entire reality takes place in the closed theatre of your brain. It feels like a fantasy fever dream. Now and then solid dramas intervene. And each year is like a twelve-step program. Each month is like a step. We watch out for August. August can be real hard ..."

"You know what, Wayne? Shut up."

Six-Day Forecast for Andrew

I

Today you will encounter the notion about accepting
things as they are.

Translated, this means that no matter how many
times you ask Bear to build you a rocket ship, he won't
build you a rocket ship. He's a dog. He'll bring you the
parts but that's as far as he'll go.

And without a rocket ship you won't be blasting off
to the International Space Station anytime soon. You're
disappointed, but there it is. Cite personal and family
reasons for this. Say your intentions have changed.
That the summer's too hot. That the last four years
have constituted a marked slump for you but it's over
now. Say you've been acting like a neural pathway, one
that's gone awry.

2

Today you will get a message from God.

God, you believe, is like one of those people who
goes up to every dog in the world and kisses it on the
mouth. He loves everyone that much.

God's message will arrive while you're driving
home and feeling great because Machine Head is
playing on the car radio. There'll be a six-pack and a bag
of taco chips on the seat beside you. You'll notice birds
flying across sunset clouds and you will suddenly think,
"Hey, that's beautiful!"

This is when God will speak to you. His voice
will seem to come from inside your body, somewhere
around your chest.

God will say, "God is dead and his mother is Mary."

God will say, "If you want to forget the sky and
the heaving earth, and human passions, and the flight
of years, try at least to remember that your presence
once cast a shadow here and also that, however muted,
you were filled with a light that can only be described
as radiant."

3

Today you're thinking you don't want to be a recycler
forever, that eventually you'll become an entrepreneur
and own your own recycling-equipment plant.

You're like the actor Steve Buscemi, you think, a guy
who is always playing himself in a movie. You're feeling
that authentic.

Probably, you drink too much. You admit it. But you
have a willingness to never let a friend drink alone. You
use booze, you say, to heighten your good times or really
deepen your bad times, depending on where you're
lodged in your cycle of ups and downs.

Your biggest dread is that your face will be one of
those faces the world never sees, that you will never walk
a red carpet. You dreamed about this last night. You were
at the recycling plant and your pal Vincent kept burying
you in empty pop cans.

4

Your mother will call you at work this morning and say
she can no longer remain silent. You are not a lawyer,
a doctor, a teacher, or an investment advisor. You have
a diploma in Hospitality but you're working at Galaxy
Recycling sorting bottles and cans. What kind of
a future is that?

Tell her it's not a future, it's a present. That there is always a spin on the world that plays with our expectations. That you're treating all the successes and failures in your life up to this point as boot camp.

5

In alchemy, you've heard, you add water to thoughts. This makes a mind. Today, however, you are without water, and very tired. Satiny gleams of imagination are frankly absent, and so is your mind. You're hungover and would rather sleep.

You're wishing you had better skills to handle this situation because you want your life to be as good as love. It's not that your mind is empty, it's just that today it's a lost outline. The pages of your internal book are not turning.

Last night when that girl in the downstairs apartment said, "Oh Andrew, you were so good!" you didn't believe her. But really, she was just trying to be helpful as you stumbled from her couch.

6

Today, you're feeling you have a new dimension in your life. You feel good about yourself.

On your lunch break you will call your mom and say, "Things are looking up. I might be getting a promotion driving truck."

"That's wonderful, Andrew. Maybe next you'll get a job at head office."

"Yeah, maybe," you'll say.

In the evening, to celebrate your possible promotion, you and Vincent will gobble acid and wander the empty streets.

Things She Wouldn't Want

- a tiny backpack
- a giant to-go cup
- the smell of the subway
- True Religion jeans
- tearaway Adidas pants
- Kappa wear!
- one of those passport protectors that "travellers" use
- white eyeliner
- duck boots
- anything bejewelled, or Ed Hardy
- bacon
- food from the dollar store
- a fake tan
- has HPV been mentioned?
- mom shorts
- man Uggs
- a Pontiac or Plymouth vehicle
- a government job
- the stench of an old nightclub
- people talking their hype about marathons
- a personality that ends sentences with "gratitude"
- a life with indie rock
- a Juicy Couture velour tracksuit

- thick acrylic nails
- a creaky futon
- an itchy sweater
- chlamydia
- a hairy back
- insomnia
- rabbit stew
- platform sneakers
- a fake Louis Vuitton purse
- stilts, definitely stilts
- a man in Speedo swim trunks
- the creepy eyes of puppets
- dial-up internet
- bumps on the peen
- cancer
- mouldy herbs
- Chinese tattoo ink
- one of those minivans that resembles a DustBuster
- cargo pants
- clip-on sunglasses
- dry-cleaner hangers
- a sheetless mattress

- toe fungus
- a whistling nostril
- single-ply toilet paper
- a blanket hung up as a curtain
- a skort
- animals with eye goobers
- front bums and cheese butts
- a moth infestation
- chicken veins
- baby tees!
- bible verses printed on toilet paper
- a freaking unicycle
- ketchup water
- a bitchy resting face

Usually There Are a Lot of Goodies throughout the Day

"You're a mooch," Gina said to me.

I'd taken two empty bowls to her potluck dinner. Gina is passionate and tenacious and soulful and refused to compromise her position. "Mooch!"

So I kind of rain-danced at her. You know, that's where every bone in your body shakes. Right away Mother crawled out of my head screaming, "You dolt! You should have brought buns!"

There are over thirty million Facebook profiles of dead people and Mother is one of them.

In the taxi it felt good to be on the other side of commotion. Usually there are a lot of goodies throughout the day, but on this day they were in short supply.

There's the dad side of it, of course. And a lot of it was Uncle Phil and his Jack Nicholson impersonations. And there's my sister Jane, who has thicker hair. And Grandma Gibson who only had one hand but was still good at slapping. But, really, on this day, it was all me. I'd been wrestling with an agricultural crisis on earth and was not myself.

Organized Chaos

Joan is doing a little worship dance in her kitchen. She's quite a story. Big as a boulder. Ordinary as a fly. Ordinary as her husband's demented condition.

"I believe that compromise, trust, and a little kiss now and then will get you forty-eight years of marriage," she says across the breakfast table. A tricky idea to grasp, no question.

Their eyes meet – click, click.

And then she's like, aw, thumbs-up.

Vibe

I couldn't think of a better way to be vulnerable than
to show up naked. As a middle-class white person,
I am symbolically divesting myself of the trappings
of privilege.

Salon Day

At Barbara's House of Hair we sit before a row of
mirrors. Black capes are fastened around our necks.
Some of us sip flavoured water; others, KORA Bancha
tea. The war is over. We are done with the heavy lifting.

Even so, I can't avoid my face in the mirror.
My sagging jaw line, my limp hair. I look like my father.

At one point the young stylists holding bottles of
dye, cans of spray, packs of extensions, line up behind
us to begin their work. They look like an Apache raiding
party arranged on a cliff, come to take us down.

For distraction, Grace Kelly, the salon chihuahua,
clacks across the floor in her pink lace dress. Now and
then she jumps on a patron's lap, and when she does
you hear a chirp of joy. Otherwise we remain quiet and
well-behaved.

The Day Comes Round with Unfailing Regularity

He is flummoxed by his solid Elaine. She's in the kitchen
eating Salt 'n Vinegar chips, watching the bike race from
the kitchen window. She's singing the national anthem,
cheering the racers on.

Living with Elaine, he thinks, is like experiencing
a shark attack and a tornado at the same time.

After the race she becomes obsessed with the rats
in the attic and orders him to do something about them.
"Even the most trivial phenomenon can turn out to be
important!" she calls from the stepladder.

A while later he presents her with a dried rat
in a trap.

Now he's her favourite conqueror in the world.
"If you had died a rat advocate," she says, "if you were
a shocked, self-centred, alien, your colour faded,
I couldn't love you more!"

On a Busy Corner of Reality

A whisper in his ear and the wind chimes rustle.

A little kiss and the sky grows soft.

Love in the major leagues, you think.

You're like the sound you'd get if you plucked the cables on the Golden Gate Bridge.

You're like *Dancing with the Stars* gone local.

Any time you get to break out the tux and put on heels and eat and drink, you love it. It's like a little comedy then. A lot of pathos, some music, a tiny bit of sex off-screen.

The Cricket Problem

That chirping sound you've been hearing inside your
ears of late? It's likely a cricket infestation. House
crickets will often take up residence in the area of the
brain known as the frontal lobe. This could be your
problem. It would explain your recent lack of motivation,
a marked decrease in your dopamine levels, and
your shaming by family and friends because of your
recent behaviour.

  To determine where the crickets enter your body,
stand outside on a night when the chirping is loudest.
Most likely they are entering through your mouth.
You will need to start keeping it shut.

  If this doesn't get rid of the house crickets,
remember that they only live for three months.
They should be gone from your brain by November.
There is no guarantee, however, that your family and
friends will return in their place.

Father's Advice

If you want to succeed in finance you can't
skydive every day.

Maybe you've had enough trips to Thailand.

Maybe your long vacation is over.

Maybe you need to take a break from your self-esteem.

You have to actually go to a job and stay there for period
of time if you want to make money.

The real magic is having a savings account that grows.
In being free of the hard marching.

In two years you will be forty years old.

Hayden, I know you're in there.

Mother's Advice

Be emblematic of good things.

Try to remember you're in love with your messy life.

Find the glint, find the funny.

Think of sleep as an eight-hour hiatus.

Think of dreams as gifts from your unleashed self.

Are you getting this down?

Remember, what works best is friendship stories.

That the only bad food is food that tastes bad.

So paddle your own big shoe.

Things are actually very light and illusionary, like clouds, which are a momentary stage in the incessant cycle of rising and falling water.

When night arrives be sure to let a thousand butterflies escape from your lips.

Parting Advice

She was one hundred years old and in good shape,
considering. There was no slamming of car doors or
tears in the shepherd's pie. But on her next birthday she
said she'd had enough, she was going to kill herself.

"Okay," we said, "we just want it to be a happy
ending." We were laughing, but at something awful.

She would kill herself, she said, by not eating.
But because she made the rules, she would allow herself
one tablespoon of Scotch over ice each day.

It took three weeks. Near the end she told us
her memories were like clockwork mechanisms that
unravelled and snapped back together again.

We said, "Tell us something useful."

"About what?"

"Love."

"Oh that," she said. "Well, stay away from dolls.
Dolls are creepy. There's that stare that never changes,
that same crazy face."

"Tell us something better."

"Okay. Marry someone you never tire of looking
at. Picture them on a fridge magnet, on a lunch box,
on something you see everyday. Picture them as a poster
on the bus."

"Anything else?"

"Yes. You've never noticed? I've got this voice where
everyone thinks I'm from the South. I've got this drawl,
and I don't know how that happened. Maybe I got hit
with a barbecue rib when I came out of the womb.
Maybe I'll find out the answer when I crawl back in."

Chorus of Aging Rockers

- Melvin, shit, he's doing the meat draw at the Legion Saturday afternoons.

- Stoney's delivering papers. Gets up at four in the morning.

- Fuck.

- Well, my socks are sick. They're like a ten-year-olds. And look at my boots. You don't even have to untie them. You just pull the Velcro straps.

- You want sick? I got up one morning last week and threw up blood.

- Ha. I done that.

- I don't mind throwing up beer, and I don't mind throwing up vegetable soup. But when you throw up blood you're like Doc Holliday. You're dying.

- That gets your attention real quick.

- Yep.

- Being a failed rock star sucks.

- Yep.

Ring-ring. Ring-ring.

- Uh-oh.

- Don't answer. It's the Grim Reaper. He wants to know if I'm still having a nice day.

"Our hope is that down the line we might be able to do a simple blood test that tells if you will be a naltrexone person, an acamprosate person, or a ghrelin person."

New Year's Day

It was an odd party. At one point I said to Matt Grover over by the cheese tray, "You got pinkeye?" "No," he said. "I was up all night sobbing uncontrollably."

In the living room, Morris, the chef, was sobbing with joy about his work. This was on the couch beside the retro lamp. "I get you when you're hungry," he said. "I reach you on a physiological level. Your pupils dilate, your mouth waters, your stomach rumbles. The only other people who can do that are in the porn industry."

Light from the sunset turned the room pink, causing everyone except Lee-Ann to say it was beautiful. Lee-Ann went pale and grabbed her chest. Warren, her husband, said not to worry and gave her two sublingual Ativans. In a couple of minutes Lee-Ann stopped panting.

Warren then spoke to the few of us still standing around. He spoke like a tour guide, detached yet cheerful. "It's spirits penetrating the visible world," he said. "They originate from crystals, beautiful light. Lee-Ann is sensitive to their presence and gets spooked."

"Spirits," we said.

"That's right," Warren said.

"How many?" Brian asked.

"You never know," Warren said. "Sometimes a few, sometimes thousands."

Then around six thirty a bunch of people with those subprime mortgages just got in their cars and left. I'd never seen anything like it.

Chorus of Swans

- I don't know how people do it, how they keep their minds moving.

- You mean those who don't have a sleeping imagination?

- Oh yes.

- I feel like my psyche is about to suffer permanent slippage.

- You will grow old in your own good time. You're not going to like what happens.

- You get angst. It's like a skin-picking disorder. You can't help going there. It's a bad place, honey.

- It's like when someone says to you, "I'm sorry to hear of your diagnosis."

- It's walking into the meeting room thinking: I'll give it a shot. And leaving the meeting room thinking: I never had a chance.

- It's mothers at weddings dreaming about themselves.

- It's when you break up with your hairdresser and she actually cries.

- It's me telling the photographer not to retouch my picture but he ignored my request and gave me eyebrows anyway.

- It's realizing you like to spank somebody or you like to play with rope, and then thinking you're the only person in the world who does this. You feel so alone.

- This is super awful! I'm going to moonwalk off the stage right now!

- I'm a warrior for peace but everyone always says, "Oh sit down!" They think I'm just trying to look hot.

- Mother knows she is still the hottest gadget around. But this is not the time to tell the story because it will cause great strife. One day you'll be able to tell it.

- If you hang around long enough you're going to have a lot of stories to tell.

- One time I stole a jellybean. I was grounded for a month.

- Some of us have a cheerleader gene that's wired into our brains to keep the rest of us going.

- What keeps me going is that I'm part of a memory base for someone else's life – and hopefully that's a good thing, and hopefully they're good memories.

- Some of us might look like swans but we're paddling furiously under water.

Eternity Delayed

It's a different story this year. You don't run away from
it. You arrive on time for your annual deviation from the
norm. You are ready.

    You have trained in the uses of the dream catcher,
as did Joseph Cornell. But it's taking a lot out of you.
It's like being boxed with a stuffed canary, an hourglass,
a piece of string, and a blue egg. The air's so rare.
Outside chatter has ceased to exist.

    And you are still basically an awkward kid.
Your visits to the writing desk are often noxious, though,
now and then, goodwill flows your way. Regard and
money. This is health.

    Your only worry is whether or not your characters
will show up for duty. They seldom do. You'll be their
stand-in again.

    Your only hope is that the word-police will keep
mountains from falling on your vigilance. That people
will think of champagne and Liza Minnelli when
they read you.

The Chorus Discussing God

- He's an artist who thinks in public. He'll help us think beyond the end of the world.

- His world vanished long before we ever entered it, but he certainly sustained the take-charge illusion with remarkable grace.

- He shaped and gave a kind of consensus to how we see the world.

- A world filled with clichés. And when you get to the guts of those clichés, you realize you know almost nothing about them.

- There's a story here that we're just not seeing.

- I've heard that God created the world to fend off boredom. He had nothing else to do.

- I've heard he gives great parties. The mood is upbeat.

- More like a savage journey of the heart, in my opinion.

- We're supposed to have asked, "We have to do this with clothes?" He's supposed to have answered, "You figure out how to do it with clothes."

- Ever since, women are scurrying and guys are doing Super Mario Bros.

- Every morning we repeat the question: "What am I going to wear today?"

- You can wear whatever the hell you want as long as you kick ass.

- I do know that things are cyclical and that it's very tough for God to stay relevant for any length of time.

- I think, finally, we're just sounds.

It happens that a cricket enters an abandoned house at the end of a road rarely traveled to sing as the night is falling.

—Charles Simic

Notes

Father's Advice *(page 31)*, *second quote: Bruce McCulloch, Postmedia interview*

Today's Mystery *(page 54)*, *Banksy quote: Associated Press*

The Marilyn Statue *(page 55)*, Forever Marilyn, *by Seward Johnson*

Six-Day Forecast for Andrew *(page 91)*, *first quote: David Markson, The Last Novel*

Vibe *(page 107)*, *quote: Canadian Press, January 1, 2015*

Acknowledgments

Portions of this book were first published in *Geist, The Exile Book of Canadian Comedy, Write – The Magazine of The Writer's Union of Canada*, and the Leacock Museum's tribute anthology, *50+Poems for Gordon Lightfoot*, to whose editors grateful acknowledgment is made.

A special thank-you to Karl Siegler for once again invaluable editorial advice; to Kevin Williams, Ann-Marie Metten, and the wonderful team at Talon; and to Anna Farrant for input on "Things She Wouldn't Want."

Grateful thanks to the Canada Council for the Arts for financial support, and to the jurors who made that decision.

About the Author

Author photo by Laura Sawchuk

M.A.C. Farrant is the award-winning author of numerous works of fiction, non-fiction, memoir, and plays, and is a regular book reviewer for the *Vancouver Sun*.

The World Afloat: Miniatures, a collection of very short fiction, was published by Talonbooks in 2014 and won the City of Victoria Butler Book Prize.

Farrant lives in North Saanich, British Columbia.